Chapter One
Pixies in the Park

"Today we are finally going to trick Hinky Pink," said Violet Briggs. "I can feel it."

Violet's cousin Leon yawned. "I don't feel anything," he said. He slumped down on a green park bench. "I'm bored."

A tiny fairy popped out of Violet's pocket. He had pale green skin and tilted eyes.

"Pixie tricking is hard work, Leon," he said. "It takes time."

Violet smiled at the fairy. She still couldn't believe she knew Sprite. He had

come through the oak tree in her backyard. He told her that fourteen troublemaking fairies had escaped from his world. Sprite needed Violet's help to trick them and send them back home.

Violet had agreed to help. Then Leon found out about Sprite. Together they had tricked eleven pixies so far.

"We only have three more pixies to trick, Leon," Violet said. "Hinky Pink should be easy. We already know he can change the weather."

"So what are we doing in this park?" Leon asked.

"It's a beautiful, sunny day," Violet said. "I know Hinky Pink will try to ruin it. He'll probably make it rain or snow or something."

Sprite flew out of Violet's pocket. He landed in a nearby bush.

"Sprite! What if someone sees you?" Violet asked.

"They'll think I'm a butterfly," Sprite said, flapping his rainbow wings. "Besides, I need to look in the book."

A small bag hung from Sprite's waist. Sprite took a tiny book from the bag.

Violet knew that book. It was the *Book of Tricks*. It told how to trick the pixies.

"How do we trick Hinky Pink, anyway?" asked Leon.

"Here's the rhyme," Sprite said. He read from the book.

"'Hinky Pink can make it thunder,
He'll make it rain or hail or
  snow.

But if he tells the truth about the
   weather,
Then back home he will have to go.'"

Leon looked puzzled. "'Tells the truth about the weather'?"

"That's what it says," Sprite replied.

"How are we supposed to make him do that?" Leon asked.

Violet sighed. Leon was always complaining. "We'll figure it out," she said. "We always do."

"And if we don't, then I'll save the day," Leon said. "As usual."

Violet's face flushed red. Leon was always taking credit for things, too. He had tricked some of the pixies by accident. But he acted like he knew what he was doing all along.

Sprite tried to smooth things over. "We all work together," he said. "We're a team."

"Sprite, shhhh!" Violet said. A man was walking past the park bench. He had bright red hair and a pointy nose. He wore a coat with clouds and lightning all over it.

"Oh, my," Violet said under her breath. She whispered to Sprite, "I think that's Hinky Pink!"

Violet knew that the man was really a pixie, but Leon did not.

The man smiled and nodded at Leon. "Good afternoon," he said.

"Hi," Leon said. "Nice weather we're having, isn't it?"

The man smiled. "Why, yes," he said. "Yes, it is."

Suddenly, a tunnel of wind appeared be-

hind the man. Swirling winds pulled the shocked man into the tunnel.

Then he vanished.

"Whoa!" Leon said, jumping up. "What just happened?"

"I think you tricked Hinky Pink," Violet said. When a pixie was tricked, a wind tunnel always came to send the pixie back to the Otherworld.

"How'd I do that?" Leon asked.

Violet thought. "You got him to say that it's a nice day," she said. "You got him to tell the truth about the weather!"

Leon beamed. "Looks like I saved the day again!"

Violet cringed. She hated to admit it. But Leon had tricked Hinky Pink, fair and square. Even if it was an accident.

"Let's look in the *Book of Tricks*," Violet said. "If you really tricked him, his picture will be there now."

Violet walked to the bush where Sprite was hiding. "Sprite? Do you have the book?"

There was no answer.

Violet pushed aside leaves and branches. Sprite had to be there somewhere.

"Sprite?" Violet called. "Where are you?"

Violet spotted something on the ground. It was Sprite's magic bag.

Sprite never went anywhere without his magic bag.

Goose bumps popped up on Violet's arms. Sprite wasn't answering her. Violet and Leon couldn't find him anywhere. And his magic bag was on the ground all by itself.

That could mean only one thing.

"Oh, no, Leon," Violet said slowly. "I think Sprite is missing!"

Chapter Two
Kidnapped!

Two hours later, Leon and Violet were still searching around the park. "Violet, we've looked everywhere," Leon complained. "Sprite's not here."

Tears filled Violet's eyes. Sprite was her best friend. She didn't want anything bad to happen to him.

"Maybe he saw another one of the escaped pixies and chased after it," Leon said.

"Without telling us?" Violet asked. "That's not like Sprite at all."

Leon tried again. "Maybe he's back home, waiting for us."

"Maybe," Violet said. But something inside her told her that wasn't true.

Violet and Leon walked home to the yellow house that they both lived in. Leon and his mom, Violet's aunt Anne, lived on the first floor. Violet lived on the second floor with her mom and dad.

Violet went straight to the backyard. Sprite loved to smell the flowers there.

"Sprite," Violet called softly. "Are you here?"

A bird chirped in the old oak tree. The toad that lived in the yard croaked.

But there was no sign of Sprite.

Violet sat down with her back to the oak tree.

"What do we do now?" Leon asked.

Sprite's magic bag dangled from Violet's fingers.

"Maybe the *Book of Tricks* can help," Violet said. She took out the tiny book and flipped through it.

"There's Hinky Pink's picture," Violet said. "You really did trick him, Leon."

Violet looked some more. "There are only two rhymes left to solve. We just have to trick Finn the Wizard. And Spoiler."

"Did somebody say my name?" a voice said.

Violet gasped as a fairy appeared in front of them. Spoiler's dark hair was tied in two pigtails on top of her head. She wore a yellow-striped shirt and overalls.

"Spoiler!" Violet cried. "I should have guessed. What did you do to Sprite?"

Spoiler smiled sweetly. "Me?" she said innocently. "I didn't do anything!"

"Then who did?" Leon asked.

Spoiler waved a finger in the air. The

Book of Tricks flew out of Violet's hands and landed on the grass. The pages magically flipped until they stopped on one page.

"Finn the Wizard!" Violet read from the book. "What would he want with Sprite?"

"The wiz has got a big day tomorrow," Spoiler said. "He didn't want Sprite to spoil things for him."

"You're the only one who spoils things," Violet said angrily. She turned to Leon. "Sprite's been kidnapped! We've got to save him."

Spoiler shrugged. "I'm here to give you some advice. Don't try to find Sprite. You don't want to mess with Finn!"

"Tell us where he is!" Leon demanded.

Spoiler laughed. "No way. By tomorrow, the wiz will be mayor of this town. And there's nothing you can do to stop him."

Then she threw some glittering pixie dust over herself.

Leon and Violet ran to Spoiler. They dived after her, trying to stop her.

They were too late. Spoiler vanished.

Leon brushed the dirt from his jeans. He looked at Violet. "So," he said. "What do we do now?"

Chapter Three
Trick That Wizard!

"We've got to find Finn and trick him," Violet said. "Then we can get Sprite back."

"But how do we do that?" Leon asked. "Sprite is the Royal Pixie Tricker, remember? And he's not around."

Violet opened up the magic bag and took out a tiny medal. The words Royal Pixie Tricker were stamped on a gold circle.

Queen Mab, ruler of the fairies, had

made Sprite a Royal Pixie Tricker. He was very proud of that, even if he didn't get everything right all the time.

"I know we're not Royal Pixie Trickers," Violet said. "But we're Sprite's helpers. We've learned a lot about tricking pixies. We can do it."

Violet sat down on the green grass. She looked through the *Book of Tricks* once again.

"Here it is," Violet said. "Finn's rhyme. It will tell us how to trick him."

Violet read from the book.

"Finn will try
To keep you apart.
You must stay strong
And follow your heart.'"

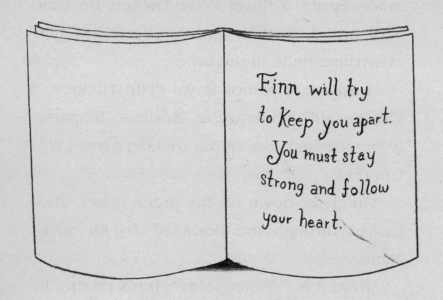

Finn will try
to keep you apart.
You must stay
strong and follow
your heart.

Leon took the book from her. "That's all?" Leon asked. "That rhyme is not much help at all."

"It's sort of helpful," Violet said. "It says we have to stay strong. And follow our hearts."

Leon frowned. "But how is that going to trick him? Usually it's pretty clear what we have to do. Like when we had to make Rusella eat alphabet soup. Or when we had to scare Buttercup. But this doesn't make sense at all."

Violet hated to agree with Leon. But she was worried, too.

Just then, Aunt Anne stuck her head out of the door to the backyard.

"Violet! Leon!" she called. "Dinner's in a half hour. We're eating early tonight."

"How come, Mom?" Leon asked.

Aunt Anne stepped into the yard. "Tomorrow's election day." She turned to Violet. "Your mom and I are going to campaign for Wiz Finnster."

Violet got chills at the sound of the name.

Wiz Finnster was the same man as Finn the Wizard. If he won the election, the whole town would be under his spell!

"You mean you like Wiz Finnster?" Violet asked. "I thought you were going to vote for Mayor Jean again. She's a great mayor."

Aunt Anne got a dreamy look in her eyes. "Wiz Finnster is the best person for the job. He said he'll work magic to make this town great. I believe he will!"

Violet recognized the look in her aunt's eyes. It was the look people got when they were under a fairy spell.

Violet looked at Leon. He saw it, too.

"I think the whole town's going to vote for Wiz Finnster tomorrow," Aunt Anne continued. "He's charmed everyone in Oakville."

"I'll bet he has," Violet muttered.

"We're going to play outside some more," Leon told his mom. "We'll come inside in time for dinner."

"Don't be late!" Aunt Anne said.

Aunt Anne shut the door behind her.

"I forgot election day is tomorrow," Violet said. "I guess that's what Spoiler meant when she said tomorrow was the wizard's big day."

"This doesn't sound good," Leon said.

Violet nodded. "We have to do more than save Sprite. If Finn wins this election, he'll take over the whole world next. He'll put everyone under a fairy spell. We'll all have to do whatever he says!"

Chapter Four
The Gnome Knows

"I don't know," Leon said nervously. "Couldn't we just let Finn win the election? Then maybe he'll let Sprite go."

Violet sighed. "We don't know that for sure. Sprite could be in danger. We have to stop Finn, Leon. We have to try."

"I guess," Leon said. Then he smiled. "Hey, maybe that queen lady can help us."

"You mean Queen Mab," Violet said. She looked inside the magic bag. "That's not a bad idea. She's helped us before. She'll know what to do."

Violet picked up a tiny purple stone. When they'd needed help before, the stone would glow. Then the queen would appear.

"Please, Queen Mab," Violet whispered. "We need you."

But the stone did not change.

Violet rubbed the stone between her hands. She held it up in the sunlight.

The queen did not appear.

"Maybe it only works for Sprite," Violet said.

Leon frowned. "Who's going to help us now?"

Violet thought about what they had done before when they needed help. It was hard to know what to do without Sprite there.

Then she remembered. Queen Mab had

once sent them to someone in the human world. Maybe he could help them again.

Violet marched out of the yard. "Let's go!" she called behind her. "I know who can help us. We'll be back before dinner."

Leon ran after her.

The last time Violet and Sprite had a problem, they went to see Robert B. Gnome. Robert looked like an ordinary garden gnome. But he was really a fairy who lived in the human world. He had helped Sprite and Violet trick Bogey Bill and Buttercup.

Robert B. Gnome lived in a garden just a few blocks away. Violet walked into the yard. She saw the small statue standing in front of a rosebush. The statue was a smiling little man with a white beard. His two arms were raised in the air. He wore a red cap on his head.

Violet knelt down in front of the gnome. "What are you doing?" Leon asked. "Are you crazy? This is just a garden gnome. It's not real!"

Violet forgot that Leon had never met the gnome before. "Trust me," she told Leon.

She turned to the statue. "Hello, Mr. Gnome," Violet whispered. "It's me, Violet. I need your help. Sprite's in trouble!"

Robert B. Gnome stood still. But Violet saw one eyebrow lift up. The gnome looked at Leon.

"Oh, he's my cousin," Violet explained. "It's okay. He knows all about Sprite."

Robert B. Gnome lowered his arms. He turned to Violet. "Sorry about that. I have to be careful around strangers. What's this about Sprite?"

Violet told Robert B. Gnome how Finn had kidnapped Sprite.

"We're not sure how to find him," Violet said. "We're not even sure how to trick Finn!"

Robert B. Gnome looked thoughtful. "Finding him shouldn't be too hard."

Robert B. Gnome took off his cap and pulled out a small corncob pipe. He put the pipe to his lips.

"Let's see what we can see," said the gnome.

Robert B. Gnome blew into the pipe, and a shimmering bubble came out of the end. The bubble grew bigger and bigger, until it was almost as large as Violet's head.

"Cool!" Leon said.

Rainbow colors swirled on the surface of the bubble. But Violet saw something else, too. Something inside.

Violet moved closer.

A scene was playing inside the bubble. Finn the Wizard was standing in a room, dressed in his wizard robes. A banner that

read WIZ FINNSTER FOR MAYOR hung across the room.

"It's Finn's Election Headquarters!" Violet said.

"Look closer," said the gnome.

Finn was in front of a golden birdcage on a stand. A black crow sat on top of the cage. But something fluttered and jumped inside it, too.

"Hey!" Leon said. "Is that —"

"Sprite!" Violet cried.

The bubble burst.

"It was Sprite in that cage!" Violet said. "Finn's got Sprite trapped in his headquarters."

Robert B. Gnome put the pipe back in his cap. He put the cap back on his head.

"Well, now you know where to find him," said the gnome.

"But what do we do when we get there?" Leon asked. "And how do we trick Finn?"

The gnome smiled. "Just follow your heart, and you will do just fine."

Robert B. Gnome raised his arms and stood still as a statue once again.

"That wasn't much help," Leon said as they walked away.

"Yes, it was," Violet said. "We know where to find Sprite. Let's go home. We need to come up with a plan!"

Chapter Five
Mallsay Inytay!

"Leon, are you awake?" Violet tiptoed into her cousin's room the next morning.

Leon tugged on a sock. "Yeah. I'm almost ready," Leon replied.

Leon pulled a brush over his messy blond hair. He looked exactly the same when he was done.

"It's a good thing school is closed for election day," Violet said. "I told our moms that we were going to work on a school project together. Now we just have to get to Finn's headquarters and save Sprite!"

"The headquarters is all the way across town," Leon said. "How are we going to get there?"

Violet took the magic bag from her pocket. "We can use pixie dust," she said. She picked up some of the shiny dust with her fingers.

Leon looked suspicious. "I thought only Sprite could use that," he said.

"He never said we couldn't," Violet said. "Besides, it's an emergency."

"Okay, but be careful. Who knows where we could end up," Leon said. He stood next to Violet. "Let's go!"

Usually, Violet held her nose when Sprite used pixie dust. It made her sneeze. But today she needed both hands.

Violet sprinkled the dust over them both.

"To Finn's election headquarters!" Violet cried. *"Achoo!"*

Violet's skin tingled. *Please work,* Violet said to herself, closing her eyes. *Please please please!*

The tingling stopped.

"Violet! Leon!" a voice cried.

Violet slowly opened her eyes. They had

made it! They were in Finn's headquarters. Violet and Leon ran to the golden cage.

"I'm so glad to see you!" Sprite said. "I knew you'd find the magic bag. That's why I dropped it when Finn grabbed me."

"Sprite, are you all right?" Violet asked.

"I'm fine," Sprite said bravely. "I'm not hurt. Just trapped. The key to the cage is over there." Sprite pointed to a hook on the wall.

The large crow perched on top of the cage ruffled its feathers. It looked at Violet with its yellow eyes.

"Caw! Caw!" screeched the crow.

"Sssssh!" Violet told it. She ran to the key.

"Hurry!" Sprite called after her. "Finn will be back any —"

Sprite's green face got pale. Violet turned around.

A tall man stood in the doorway. He had a long white beard. He wore a purple robe covered with moons and stars. He carried a long staff made out of wood. On top of the staff was a glittering crystal ball.

"Look out! It's Finn!" Leon cried, a little too late.

"Violet. Leon. What a pleasure to meet you," the wizard said. His words were friendly, but his voice sounded icy cold.

Violet spun around. She had never felt more afraid. But she bravely stepped forward. "Finn, we're here to rescue Sprite," she said. "Please let us take him with us."

Finn raised a white eyebrow. "Why? So you three can ruin my plans? You've already tricked my followers and sent them back home. No, no. I don't think letting Sprite go is a good idea at all."

The wizard smiled a wicked smile. He raised his staff in the air.

"Uh, we'll be happy to go now, sir," Leon said, taking a step backward. "We don't want to cause any trouble."

"I'll make sure that you don't," said Finn.

He pointed the staff at Leon. The crystal ball shone with white light.

"Mallsay inytay!" Finn said in a thundering voice.

A light flashed.

Violet gasped.

Leon was still there. But he was as small as Sprite!

"Hey, what happened?" Leon asked in a squeaky voice.

"Your turn," Finn told Violet.

"No!" Violet cried. Her mind raced. She thought of all the ways she knew to stop fairy magic. She didn't have on a sweater, so she could not turn it inside out. Instead, she muttered Finn's name backward under her breath.

"Nnif, nnif, nnif!" she said desperately.

Finn just smiled. He pointed the wand at her.

"Mallsay inytay!" he yelled.

The next thing Violet knew, she was standing next to Leon. Finn towered above them like a giant.

The wizard leaned down and picked them up in his wrinkled hand.

"Much better. Don't you agree, Old Tom?" Finn said, looking at the big black bird on the cage.

The wizard took the key from its hook. He opened the golden cage. Then he put Violet and Leon inside.

Violet rattled the cage bars.

"You can't do this!" she yelled. "We'll stop you. We'll find a way!"

"I wish I could stay and chat," replied the

wizard. "But I'm expected at a press conference. Old Tom, you keep an eye on them."

"Caw! Caw!" the crow screeched.

"My mom will come looking for me!"
Leon shouted. "She'll find us and let us go."

Finn's cold eyes gleamed.

"Your dear mother is under my spell," he
said. "And soon, the rest of the human world
will be, too!"

Chapter Six
Help from the Queen

Finn turned and left the room, his robes swirling behind him.

"You can't do this!" Violet yelled after him.

Then she looked down. The floor looked like it was miles away.

Suddenly, Violet felt dizzy. She sat down on the bottom of the cage.

Sprite knelt beside her. "Violet, are you all right?" he asked.

Violet looked into Sprite's eyes. She was used to being so much bigger than the fairy. He could sit on her shoulder, or rest in the palm of her hand. But now they were the same size.

"It feels a little strange," Violet said. "Everything looks so big!"

Sprite shrugged. "It looks normal to me. But I guess I'm used to it."

"Being small isn't so bad," Leon said. "Imagine if we ordered a pizza? We could eat it for a week!"

Violet had to smile. Only Leon could think of pizza at a time like this.

"Caw! Caw!" Above them, Old Tom the crow ruffled his feathers.

They looked up. From where Violet sat, the crow looked like a monster. Each of its sharp claws was as big as her head.

Leon seemed to read her thoughts. "I bet Old Tom's beak is nice and sharp, too," he said, shivering.

"Oh, Sprite!" Violet said. "We didn't know what to do without you. And now we've messed everything up."

"No, you didn't," Sprite said. "You found me. We're all together again. That's what's important."

"We still need help," Leon said.

"I know," Sprite said. "Do you still have the magic bag?"

Violet realized she had been holding the bag when Finn made her small.

"It didn't shrink with me," Violet said, handing it to Sprite. "It's the same size as always."

"Magic bags are like that," Sprite said. He

reached inside and pulled out a purple stone.

"We tried reaching Queen Mab before," Violet said. "But nothing happened."

"The stone was a special gift from Queen Mab to me," Sprite explained. "It only works when I'm around."

"That's just what I thought," Violet said.

Sprite held the stone in his hands. "Queen Mab, we need you!"

The stone looked so big now that Violet was small. She watched as it softly glowed with purple light. Then the queen appeared.

"Sprite, I see you are in trouble," the queen said in her gentle voice.

"Finn has trapped us," Sprite said. "He's made Violet and Leon small. And he's about to become the mayor of Oakville!"

"Violet and Leon found you," the queen said. "That is good."

Violet bowed to the queen. "But we're too small to do anything," Violet said. "We're helpless."

"Not so helpless as you think," the queen

replied. "There is one pixie left who can help you."

"One left?" Sprite asked. "You mean Spoiler? We tricked all the others."

The queen nodded. "Deep down, she has a very good heart."

"But she's been messing things up for us all along!" Leon protested.

The queen smiled. "Don't worry, Leon. Remember these three things," she said. "Ask Spoiler to help you. Know that it is good to be small sometimes. And don't forget to follow your heart."

The queen faded from the stone.

Chapter Seven
Help from Spoiler?

"That queen always talks in riddles," Leon complained. "Why can't she ever give us something useful? Like a magic sword or a chicken that lays golden eggs."

"Queen Mab has always given us good advice before," Violet said. "We should do what she says. We should get Spoiler to help us."

Leon took the *Book of Tricks* from the magic bag. "Maybe the queen meant we need to trick her." He flipped through the pages.

"Here it is!" Leon said.

"Spoiler's always nasty,
Or so everyone gripes.
If you want to trick her,
Ask her to change her stripes.'"

"'Change her stripes'?" Sprite wondered.

"Hey, her shirt has stripes," Leon said. "Maybe we have to get her to change her clothes. Like we did with Ragamuffin."

Violet frowned. "I don't think so. I think it's an old saying."

Sprite brightened. "Of course. Changing your stripes means that you change the way you are. You must act differently than usual."

"So we have to get Spoiler to act differently?" Leon asked. "That won't be easy."

"What won't be easy?" Spoiler asked as she appeared next to him in a puff of pixie dust.

Leon slammed the book shut. "Hey, how did you get in here?" he asked.

Spoiler blew some grains of pixie dust in Leon's face. "How do you think?"

Of course! Violet thought. *We could use the pixie dust in the magic bag to get away from Finn. We'd still be small, but at least it would be a start.*

The magic bag was right next to Spoiler's feet. Violet looked at Sprite. She could tell he was thinking the exact same thing. Violet casually walked behind Spoiler. She had to get to the magic bag.

"Not so fast!" Spoiler said. She quickly

kicked the magic bag out of the cage. It fell
to the floor below.

"Spoiler!" Violet cried.

"Caw! Caw!" cried the crow above them.

"I guess we'd better forget about Spoiler
helping us," Leon said.

Spoiler laughed. "Me! Help you? Why would I want to do that?"

"Well, we used to be friends, back in the Otherworld," Sprite said glumly. "I don't understand what happened."

Spoiler scowled. "Of course you do. It's because Queen Mab let you be a Royal Pixie Tricker and not me."

"So you decided to help Finn instead?" Violet asked. "But he's mean."

"Not to me," Spoiler said. "He lets me do important things for him."

"You mean *bad* things," Violet said.

Spoiler shrugged. "It's no big deal. I'm not hurting anybody."

Sprite's wings fluttered. "Of course you are. Look at poor Violet and Leon! Finn couldn't have done this without your help," he said.

Spoiler studied Violet and Leon. "I think their new size is an improvement," she said.

Leon slumped to the floor of the cage. "I can't believe Queen Mab said you had a good heart. She must have been talking about some other Spoiler."

Spoiler sharply turned her head. "What did you say?" she asked.

"I said Queen Mab must have been wrong about you," Leon said. "You're not nice at all."

Why does Spoiler care what Queen Mab says? Violet wondered.

"What did she say? Please tell me," Spoiler begged.

"Oh, I'm sure you don't want to hear that," Violet said. "You're so busy helping Finn. You probably don't even like Queen Mab."

Spoiler stamped her foot. "I do, too!" she said. Then she looked down at her feet. "Queen Mab just doesn't like me."

Violet was starting to get an idea why Spoiler was so mean.

"Are you sure about that?" Violet asked. "Because she did say you have a good heart."

Spoiler's eyes widened. "She did?" asked the pixie.

Violet nodded. "She said you would help us."

"Queen Mab really does like you," Sprite said. "I bet if you went back to the Other-world she'd give you a job. A good job, where you could help people."

"She likes me?" Spoiler looked like she didn't believe it.

Sprite nodded.

"Finn can be cranky sometimes," Spoiler said slowly. "And he's always making me iron his wizard robes."

"Queen Mab is never cranky," Sprite said.

Spoiler brushed a lock of hair from her face.

"I'll do it!" she said. "I'll go back to Queen Mab."

Spoiler took some pixie dust from her pocket. ·

"Hey!" Leon yelled. "Can you get us out of here first?"

"Why not?" Spoiler asked. She threw a big handful of pixie dust over them all.

Violet sneezed. The next thing she knew, they were all on the floor. The black crow was locked safely inside the cage.

"Thanks, Spoiler," Violet said. "Looks like you've changed your stripes after all!"

A wind tunnel appeared behind Spoiler. The pixie smiled as it sucked her inside.

"No hard feelings!" she cried. Then she vanished.

Chapter Eight
Finn's Bargain

"We tricked Spoiler!" Leon cried.

"And we're out of that cage," Violet said. The golden prison swung high above them.

"*Caw! Caw! Caw!*" screeched the crow in protest.

Sprite found the magic bag and strung it around his waist. "I won't lose you again," he promised it.

"Let's get out of here!" Leon said.

"Uh, there's one problem," Violet reminded him.

"What?" Leon asked.

Violet sighed.

"Oh, yeah," Leon said. "We're still small." His face brightened. "Hey, maybe we won't have to go to school anymore!"

Violet turned to Sprite. "How can we get big again?"

"Only Finn can break the spell," Sprite said. "This is strong magic."

"So we'll have to make him change us back," Leon said.

"Or trick him," Violet said. "When we tricked some of the other pixies, their magic stopped."

"I still don't know how we're supposed to do that," Leon said. "Especially since we're so small. Finn could squash us like bugs."

Violet thought, *Queen Mab was right about Spoiler. She also said that being small could be useful.*

Violet looked around the room. It was dark and creepy, with stone walls and bubbling tubes in the corner. But there were also things you would find in an office. The big banner that said WIZ FINNSTER FOR MAYOR hung across the room. A desk had tape and thumbtacks and other things on it.

An idea formed in Violet's mind. She told Sprite and Leon.

"It might work," Sprite said. "We have to hurry, though. Finn will be back soon."

"It sounds crazy to me," Leon said. "But I guess we should try."

Violet turned to Sprite. "If this works, we'll be big again. The one nice thing about being small is that we're all the same size. I like that."

Sprite's cheeks blushed bright green. "Me, too," he said, giving her a hug.

"Hey, I hear Finn coming!" Leon cried.

Leon quickly hid behind a stone pillar. Sprite picked up Violet and flew her up to Finn's desk. Then he flew to the tubes in the corner. Strange liquids bubbled inside them.

"In just a few hours, I will be mayor of this town!" Finn said, his voice booming grandly. He had changed out of his wizard robes and was wearing the suit he always wore in the human world. He still carried his staff. "Aren't you proud of me, my little captives?"

Finn peered inside the golden cage.

"Caw!" complained Old Tom.

"Drat!" Finn cried. "They've escaped!"

Leon jumped out from behind the pillar. *"Nyah! Nyah! Nyah!"* he yelled as loudly as he could. "You can't get me!"

Finn raised an eyebrow. "Oh, you like to play games, do you, little one?" He bent down and ran toward Leon.

Violet pushed one of the boxes of thumbtacks as hard as she could. The box fell off

the desk. Thumbtacks rolled all over the floor.

"What's this?" Finn cried. He stepped on one of the tacks.

"*Ow!*" Finn yelled. He hopped up and down on one foot.

Sprite knocked over some of the bubbling tubes. Liquid spilled onto the floor.

The wizard lost his balance on the slippery floor. He fell down onto a pile of thumbtacks. His staff fell from his hands and clattered across the floor.

"*Ow, ow, ow!*" Finn whined.

"Sprite, now!" Violet yelled.

Sprite flew up to the banner that read WIZ FINNSTER FOR MAYOR. He wrapped the long sheet around and around Finn's body. The wizard looked like a mummy wrapped up in the banner. He couldn't move.

Violet breathed a sigh of relief. Being small was useful. Finn was trapped. Now he just might change them back.

Finn's eyes turned an angry shade of red. "I'll get you all! I'll send you to the Sahara Desert! Or maybe I'll turn you into earthworms. I'm sure Old Tom would like a little snack."

"*Caw!*" The crow seemed to like that idea.

Finn looked at the crystal on his staff. The crystal began to glow again.

A beam of light shot from the crystal. It hit the door of the birdcage. Old Tom flew out and landed next to Finn's head.

Violet groaned. She hadn't counted on this.

Suddenly, there was a loud knock on the door.

"Mr. Finnster! Mr. Finnster! We're waiting to take photos," a voice said.

Reporters, Violet guessed. *Reporters for the press conference.*

"You don't want the press to see you like this, do you?" Violet asked Finn. "They will take pictures of you."

Sprite flew to the doorknob. "I'll let them in," he threatened. "They'll see that you're a wizard. They'll expose you for what you are. Then you won't become mayor."

Finn's eyes narrowed.

"Let me make you a deal," Finn said. He looked right at Violet. "I will turn you and the boy here back to your normal size. I'll let you leave unharmed."

"What about Sprite?" Violet asked.

"I can't trust anyone who works for the queen," Finn said. "I'll keep him here with me until I become mayor. Then I'll send him back to the Otherworld where he won't cause me any more trouble."

Violet couldn't dream of leaving Sprite.

"What if we refuse?" Violet said.

The crystal began to glow again. This time, the light hit a pencil next to Violet.

Zap! The pencil turned into a wriggling worm.

Violet jumped back. She ducked behind a stapler.

Old Tom the crow flew up to the desk. He

grabbed the worm in his sharp beak and slurped it down. Then he looked right at Violet.

"Take my deal," said the wizard. "Or I'll feed you and all those reporters to Old Tom for lunch!"

Violet didn't know what to do.

If she stayed, she might be able to help Sprite.

Or she might be turned into a worm.

If she left, she and Leon would be big again. They'd be safe.

But who knew what Finn would do to Sprite?

Finn tapped his foot. "Well, little girl?" he asked. "What is your decision?"

Chapter Nine
"Follow Your Heart"

Sprite held the doorknob, ready to expose Finn. The wizard pointed his staff at Violet, ready to turn her into Old Tom's lunch.

Somebody had to make a move. And that somebody was Leon.

"Don't worry, Mr. Wizard," Leon said. "We're out of here. You don't even have to make us big." He started to run for the door.

"Leon!" Violet shouted.

Leon stopped. He looked at Violet. Then he looked at Sprite. He lowered his eyes.

"Sorry," Leon said. "I'd rather eat lunch than be somebody's lunch, that's all."

"I know," Violet said. "But we can't leave Sprite. He's our friend."

Leon nodded.

"Violet, no!" Sprite flew to her. "Finn's right. This is your only chance. I'll be happy as long as I know you're safe."

"Thanks, Sprite," Violet said. "But I'll never be happy if I leave you with Finn."

Violet stood up. She took a deep breath.

"Turn us into worms if you have to, Finn," Violet said. "I'm not leaving Sprite. No deal."

"Me, neither," Leon said. "We're a team!"

Finn grinned. "Perhaps I won't even bother to turn you into worms," the wizard said. "I think you'll make a tasty snack just as you are."

"Caw! Caw!" agreed Old Tom. The crow hopped over to Violet. He opened his long shiny beak. There was no way to escape. The crow was too big. Violet closed her eyes.

"Violet, no!" Sprite cried. He flew between Violet and the hungry bird.

Then Violet heard a noise.

A noise of swirling winds.

"Excellent!" Leon yelled.

Violet opened her eyes. A tunnel of wind, bigger than she had ever seen, was swirling above Finn. The strong winds blew papers and posters everywhere.

Finn turned around and saw the tunnel. "Nooooo!" cried the wizard.

Sprite grabbed Violet. "Hold on!" he yelled.

Old Tom was the first to go. The winds sucked the crow inside. The black bird disappeared.

Then the tunnel picked up Finn. The wizard's long legs flew behind him. All Violet could see was Finn's head. His angry eyes flashed.

"I'll get you for this!" the wizard screamed. "I'll get you all!"

Then, suddenly, all was quiet. The wizard was gone.

Violet suddenly felt strange. She looked down. Sprite was sitting in the palm of her hand.

She was big again!

So was Leon. Her cousin ran up to her and hugged her.

"We did it!" Leon yelled. "We tricked him! But I'm not really sure how."

"I think it's because we followed our hearts," Violet said. "You and I decided to stay and help Sprite. And Sprite risked his life to save me from Old Tom. That broke Finn's spell."

She looked down at the fairy. "Thanks, by the way."

Sprite smiled.

The door burst open. Men and women with cameras and notepads and microphones burst inside. They looked confused.

"Uh, could you tell us what we're doing here?" one of the reporters asked.

Sprite quickly hid behind Violet.

"You're here to interview Wiz Finnster," Violet said.

The reporters stared at her, confused.

"He's running for mayor," Violet reminded them.

"Mayor Jean is the mayor of Oakville," a reporter said. "No one's running against her."

"They don't know who Finn is," Leon whispered.

Violet nodded. Whatever spell Finn had on the town, it was over. Completely.

"I guess you'd better go home then," Violet told the reporters.

The reporters muttered among themselves. Then they headed out the door.

"Hey, I guess we saved the world, didn't we?" Leon asked. "What should we do now?"

"I think," Violet said, "we should go home!"

Chapter Ten
Good-bye, Sprite

Violet and Leon sat under the oak tree in their backyard. Sprite perched on Violet's shoulder.

Violet had the *Book of Tricks* in her hand. She had turned to the page with Finn the Wizard's rhyme.

Finn seemed to glare at them from the book. Old Tom sat on Finn's arm.

Violet shuddered. "He was the meanest

fairy yet," she said. "What will happen to him now that he's back in the Otherworld?"

"Queen Mab will probably put him in fairy prison," Sprite said.

"What if Finn tries to escape again?" Leon asked. "He escaped before, didn't he?"

Sprite sighed. He looked at Violet. "Leon's right. Finn might try to escape again.

Queen Mab needs me," he said. "I have to go back. It's my duty as a Royal Pixie Tricker."

Violet felt her stomach flip-flop. Somehow, deep down, she had known Sprite would have to leave. But she didn't want to think of it.

"But we're friends. We're a team," Violet said, trying not to cry. "Can't you please stay?"

Sprite sadly shook his head. "I belong to the Otherworld." He held up his Royal Pixie Tricker medal. "I have to go."

"We're your helpers!" Leon said. "We could go with you."

Sprite gave a little smile. "I wish you could, but the Otherworld can be dangerous for humans."

"But Violet and I can take it," Leon insisted.

"It doesn't matter," Sprite said. "You and Violet belong here. The human world needs you."

"Do you have to leave right now?" Violet asked. "We had so much fun together. I don't want you to go yet."

Sprite thought. "Well, I guess it's okay if I stay a little bit longer." He took out some pixie dust. "Are you ready for one more adventure?"

Violet and Leon nodded.

Without a word, Sprite threw the pixie dust on them.

Violet sneezed. She waited to disappear.

Instead, she found herself rising into the sky.

She looked at Leon. He was rising, too. Their feet were no longer on the ground.

"We can fly!" Violet cried.

Sprite laughed and flew in front of her face.

"It's fun, isn't it?" he said.

"It's awesome!" Leon yelled.

Up and up they went. Soon they were above the branches of the oak tree.

"Straighten your body," Sprite said, holding his arms out in front of him. "And follow me!"

A gentle breeze touched Violet as she flew after Sprite. She and Sprite and Leon were soaring over Oakville.

They flew over the garden where Robert B. Gnome kept his peaceful watch.

They flew over Leon and Violet's school,

where Bogey Bill and Buttercup had caused so much trouble.

They flew over the park, where Pix had trapped kids in a fairy ring.

They flew over the pet store, where Aquamarina had turned people into fish.

They flew over the soccer field, where Sport had enchanted a soccer team.

They flew over the woods, where Greenie and Meanie had kept their doggie zoo.

They flew and flew. Faces of the pixies they had tricked danced in Violet's head. Jolt. Ragamuffin. Fixit. Rusella. Hinky Pink. Spoiler.

Through it all, she saw Sprite's smiling face. His pointy ears. His tilted green eyes.

The sun began to set, turning the sky a beautiful shade of purple. Soon stars twinkled in the twilight.

"Good-bye, Violet," Sprite said, flying ahead of her. "I'll never forget you!"

"Sprite, wait!" Violet cried.

She sat up and rubbed her eyes.

She was at home, in her room, in bed. The morning sun streamed through the window.

"No!" Violet cried. It couldn't be!

Violet looked at the clock. It was seven A.M.

Was it all a dream?

But it all seemed so real. She had flown over Oakville with Sprite and Leon. She had helped Sprite trick the pixies. It couldn't have been a dream.

Violet sank back down into her pillows. Something small and shiny slipped out onto the floor.

Violet reached down and picked it up.

It was a Royal Pixie Tricker medal!

Violet turned it over. Her name was inscribed on the back.

Violet stared at the medal in her hand. It was all real. The medal proved it.

Leon came running into her room.

"Did you get one?" Leon asked excitedly.

He held a Royal Pixie Tricker medal in his hand. "It has my name on it."

Violet held out her hand. "Mine, too," she said.

"Cool!" Leon said. He bounced on Violet's bed. "What do you think it means?"

Violet stared at the medal. The face of a tiny pixie grinned at her.

Violet smiled. "I think it means that our pixie-tricking days have just begun!"

Pixie Tricks Stickers

Place the stickers in the *Book of Tricks*.
You can find your very own copy of the *Book of Tricks*
in the first two books of the Pixie Tricks series,
Sprite's Secret and *The Greedy Gremlin*. When Sprite
and Violet catch a pixie, stick its sticker in the book.
Follow the directions in the *Book of Tricks*
to complete each pixie's page.